Baby Lion

Story by Beverley Randell

Illustrations by Julian Bruère

Baby Lion is asleep

in the sun.

Look at the big lions.

The big lions

are in the grass.

Baby Lion wakes up.

Mother Lion is not here.

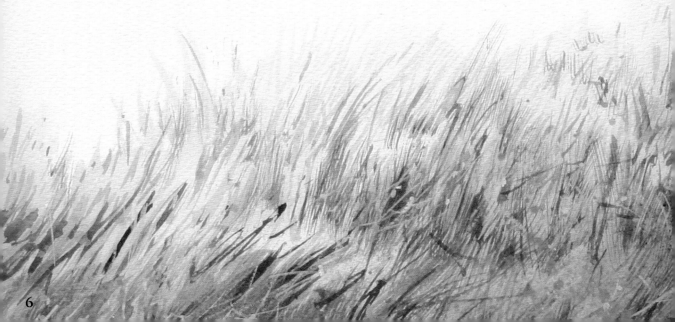

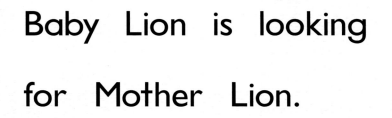

Baby Lion is looking

for Mother Lion.

Mother Lion is not here.

Baby Lion is in the grass.

Mother Lion is not here.

Here comes Mother Lion.

Baby Lion can see Mother Lion.

Look at Mother Lion.

Baby Lion is safe.